THE ADVENTURES of RUSTY Lugnut

Illustration by
MICHAEL PENTA

RONNIE'S RACECAR GARAGE

RUTH BLOWERS-MARQUART

Copyright © 2017 Ruth Blowers-Marquart
All rights reserved
First Edition

Fulton Books, Inc.
Meadville, PA

Published by Fulton Books 2017

ISBN 978-1-63338-511-5 (Paperback)
ISBN 978-1-63338-512-2 (Digital)

Printed in the United States of America

*In Loving memory
of Helen E. and Edgar J. Cottrell,
Devoted parents, grandparents,
and great-grandparents.
For always believing
that we could do anything
we set our minds to.
We miss you dearly.*

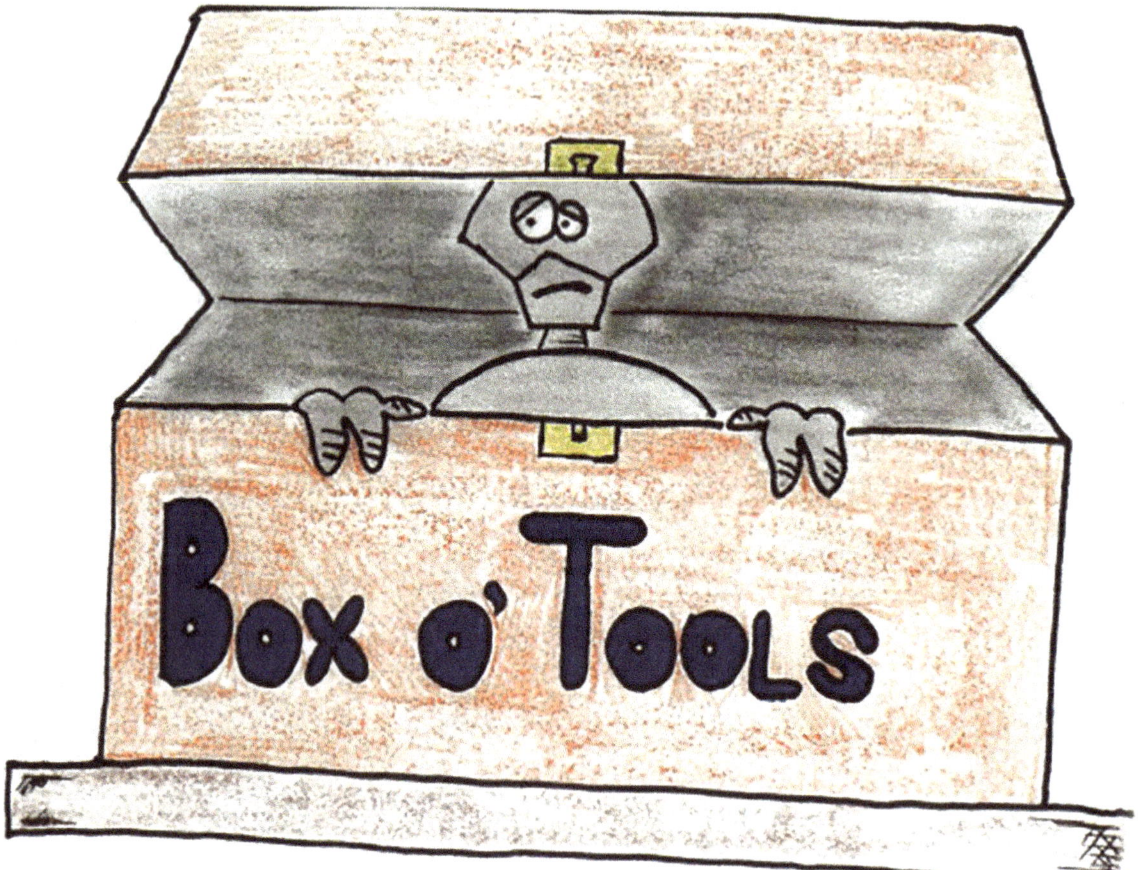
Box o' Tools

Rusty Lug Nut lived in a tool box in the busy garage of Ronnie Racecar.

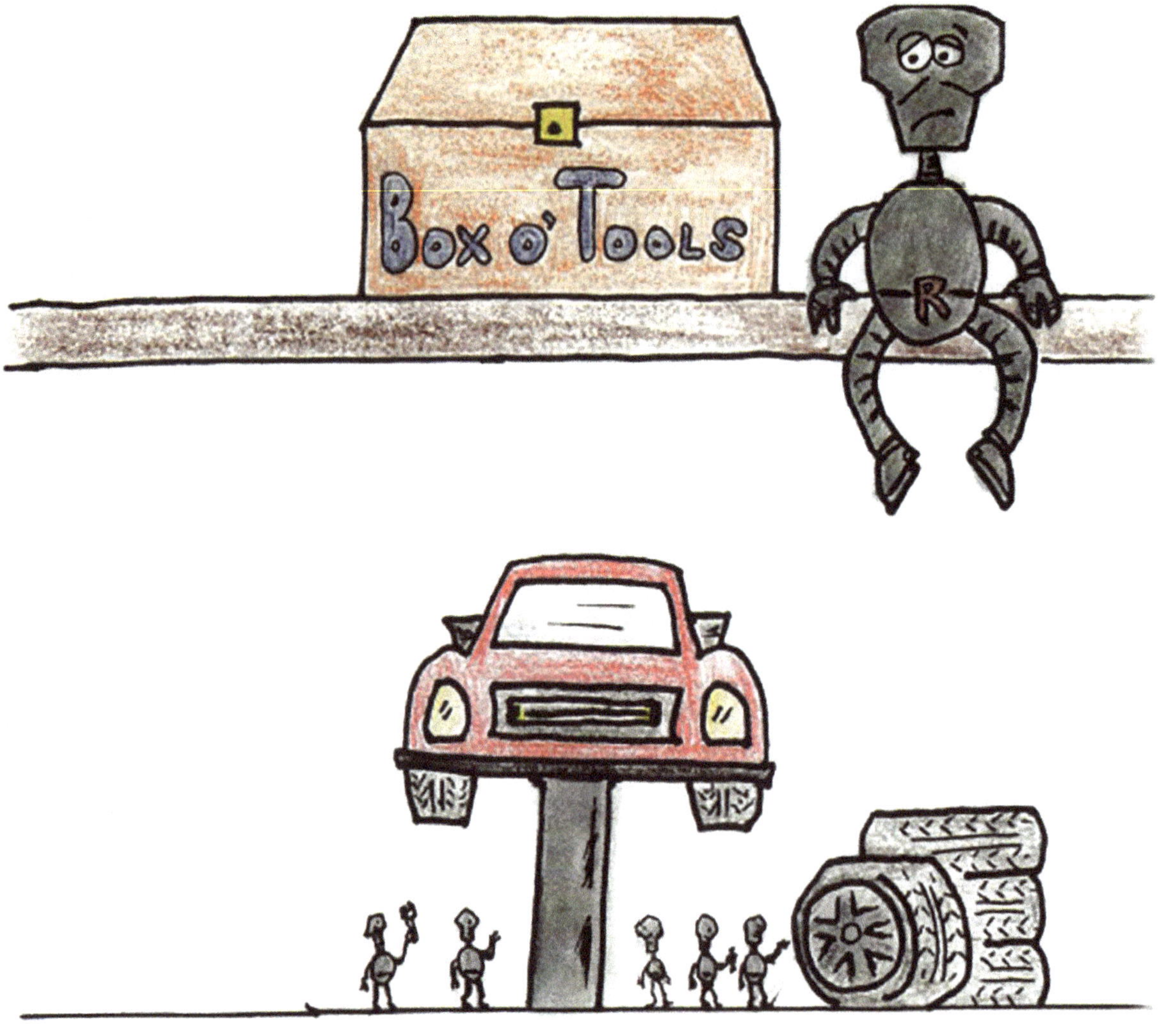
Box o' Tools
R

Every week, Rusty watched the other lug nuts work to make Ronnie's wheels go round and round and faster and faster.

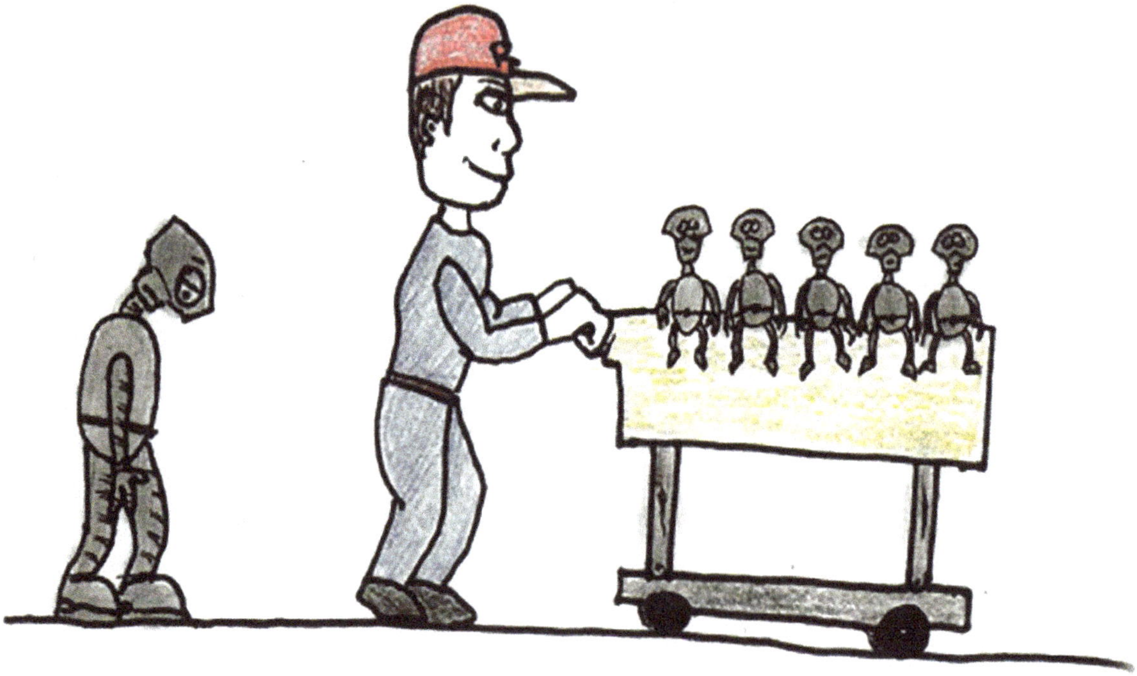

Rusty did not get chosen because he was not shiny and new like the other lug nuts. He did not look like them, and this made Rusty feel sad.

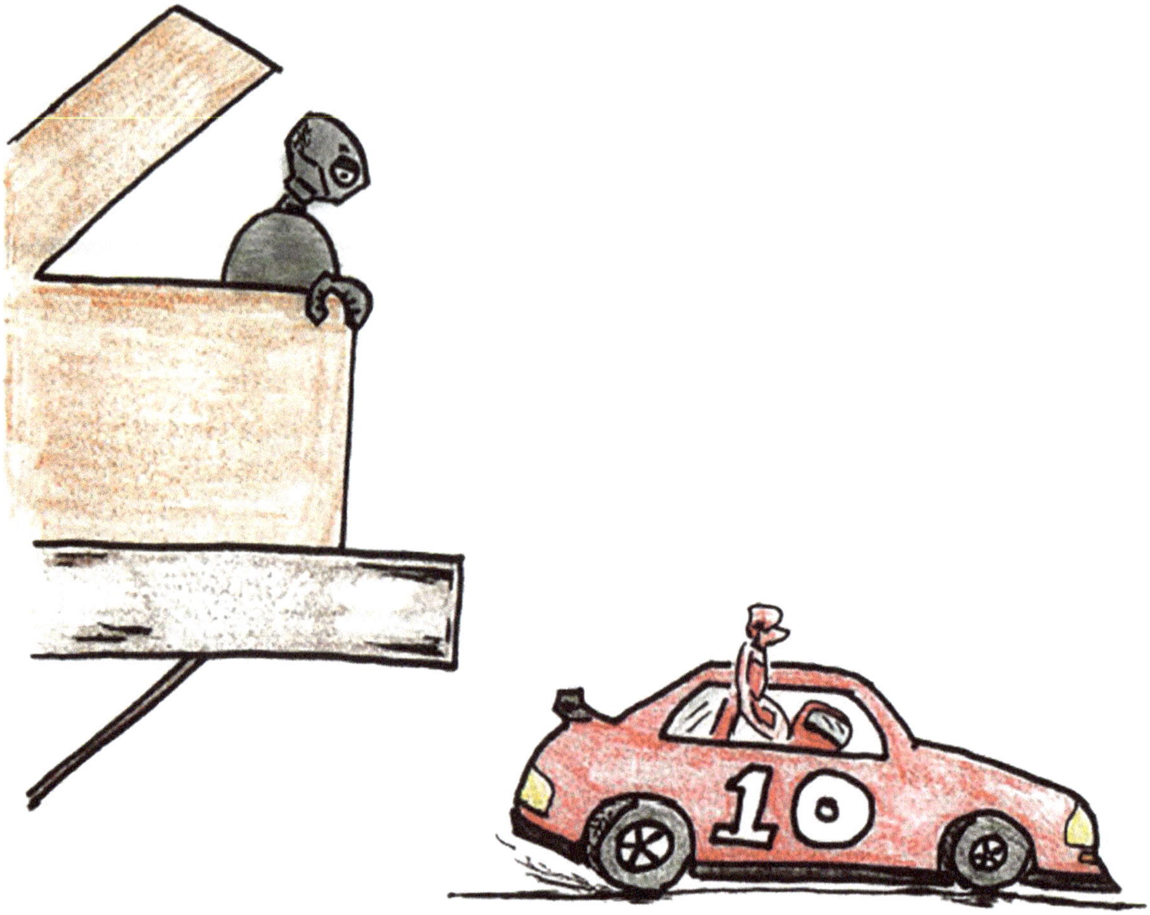
10

Ronnie's pit crew did not think Rusty could help Ronnie's wheels go round and round and faster and faster like the other shiny, new lug nuts could, so they left him all alone in the tool box. Poor Rusty!

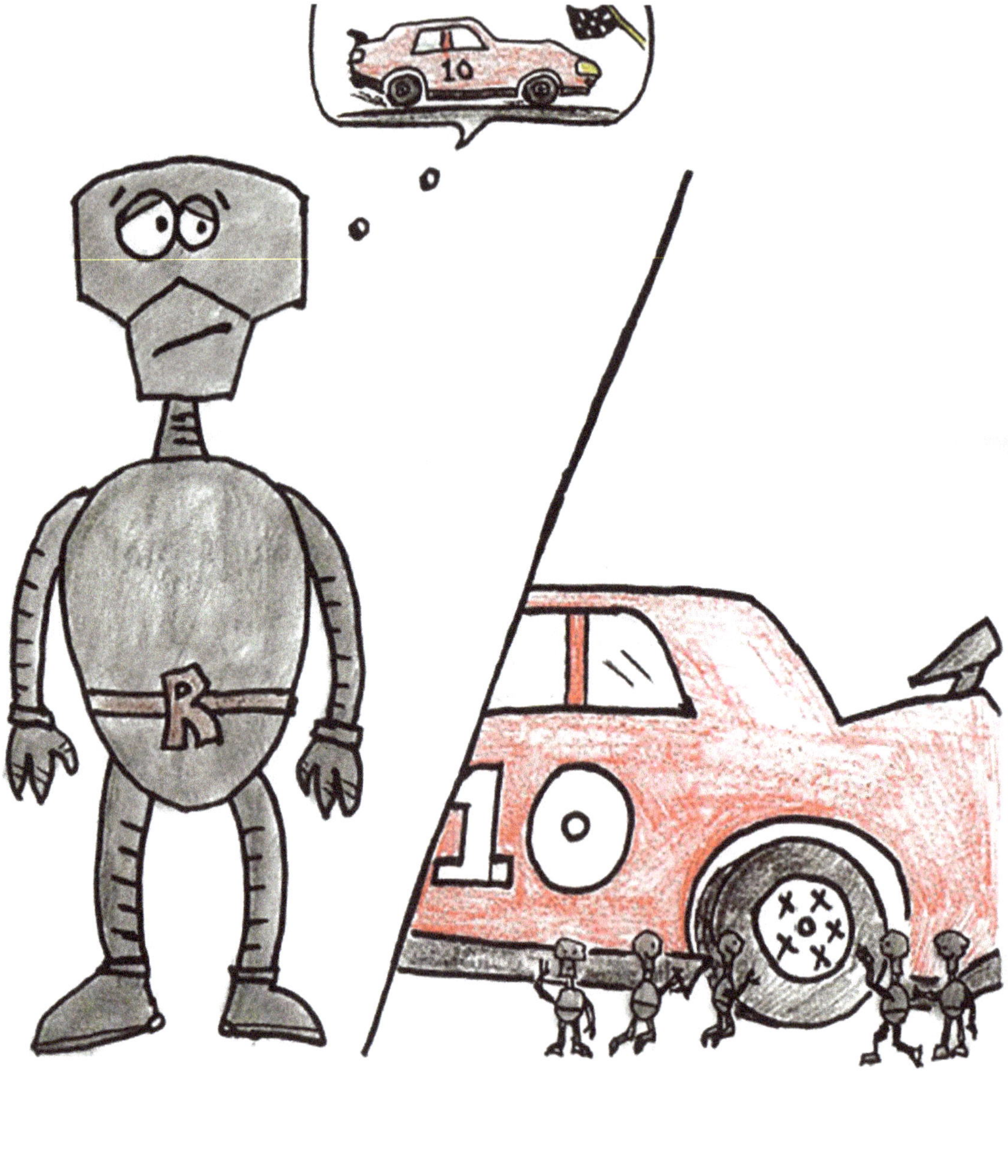
10
R
10

Week after week he watched as five other lug nuts got picked, but not him. He sat quietly and wished he could be part of the team to make Ronnie's wheels go round and round and faster and faster.

RACE DAY!
S M T W TH F S
1 2 3 4 5 6
7 8 9 10 11 12 13
14 15 16 17 18 19 20
21 22 23 24 25 26 27
28 29 30 31
10
99
39
5

So week after week, Rusty cheered loudly for Ronnie to win the race, even though Rusty did not feel like he was shiny enough to help the team. Ronnie drove fast, but he didn't win a single race.

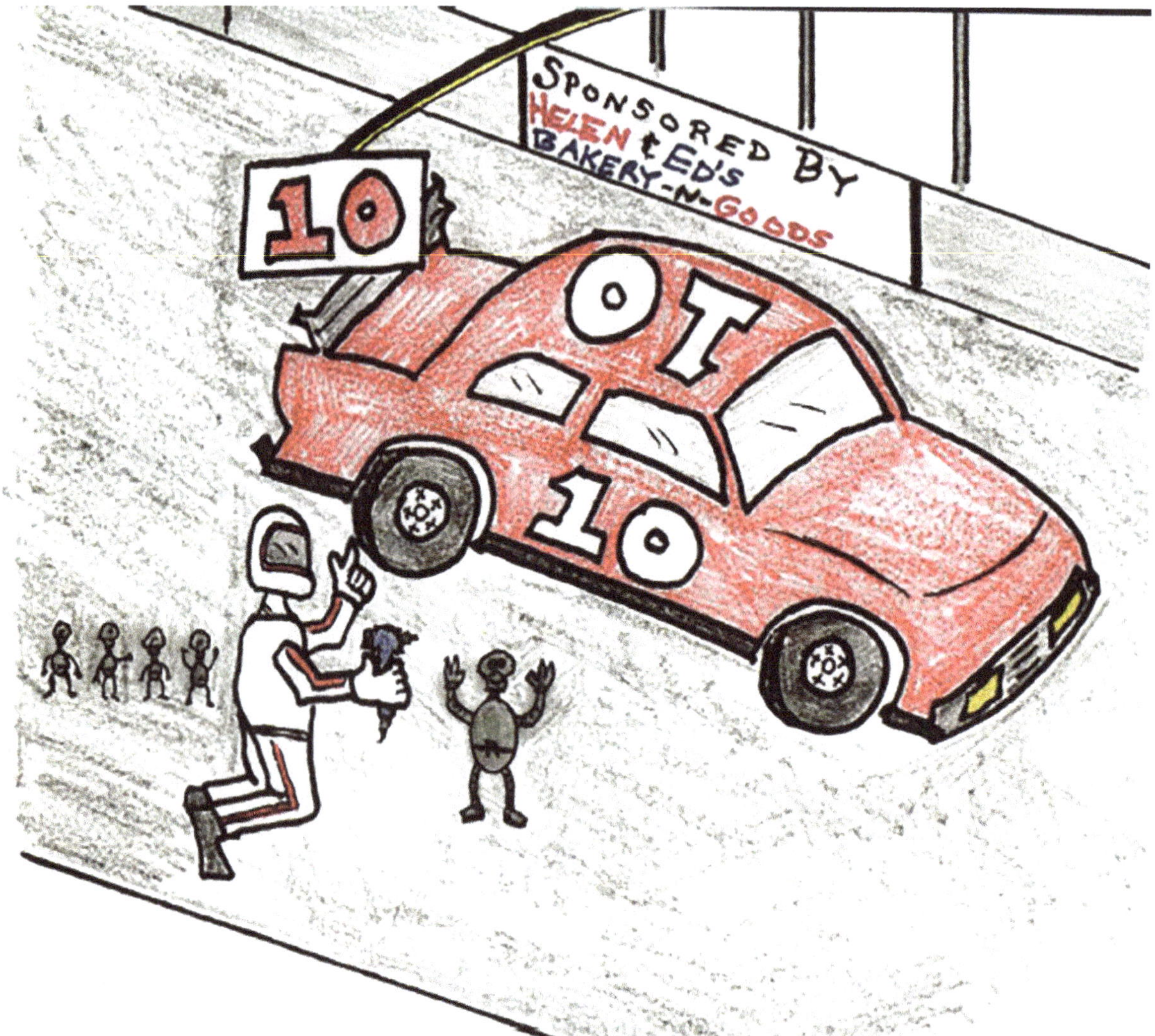
10
SPONSORED BY
HELEN & ED'S
BAKERY-N-GOODS
OT
10

Then one day, when Ronnie came into Pit Road for a tire change during the race, when the tire changer on the pit crew grabbed the shiny, new lug nuts, he grabbed Rusty too! Rusty was so happy!

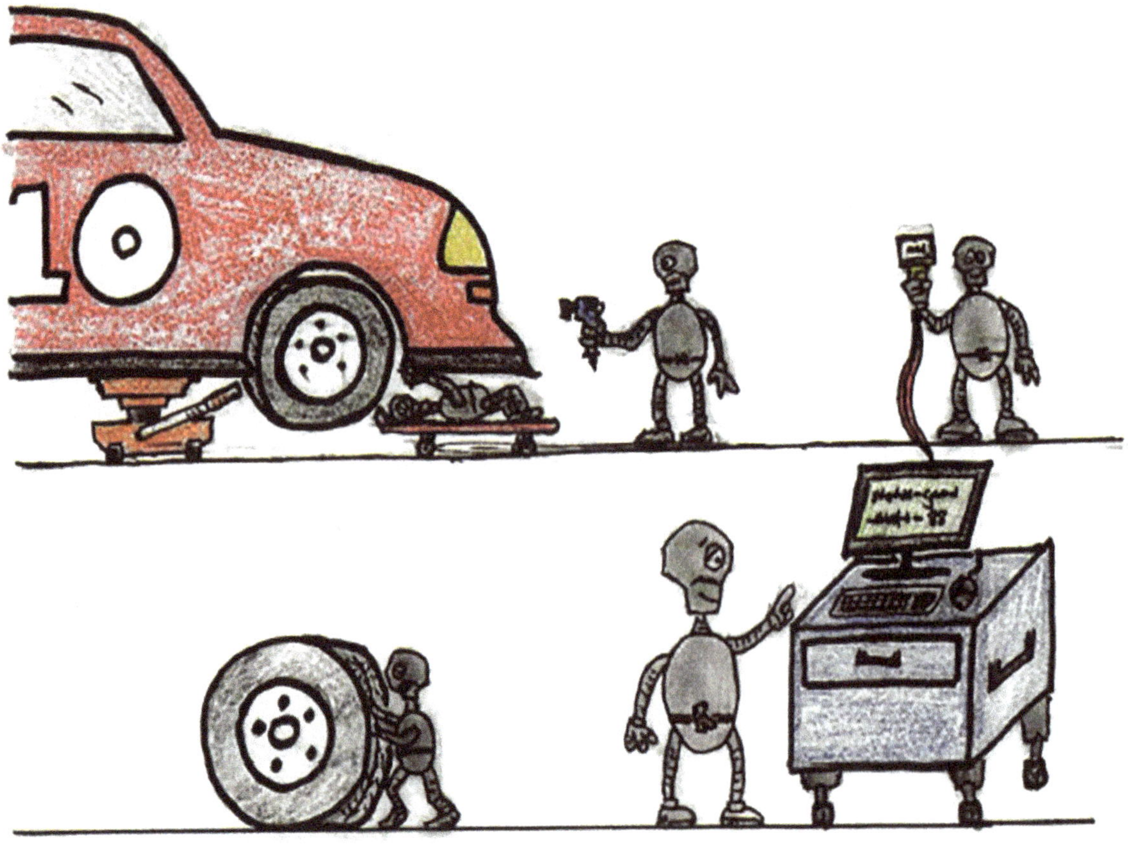

He was helping the other lug nuts
make Ronnie Racecar's wheels go round
and round and faster and faster.

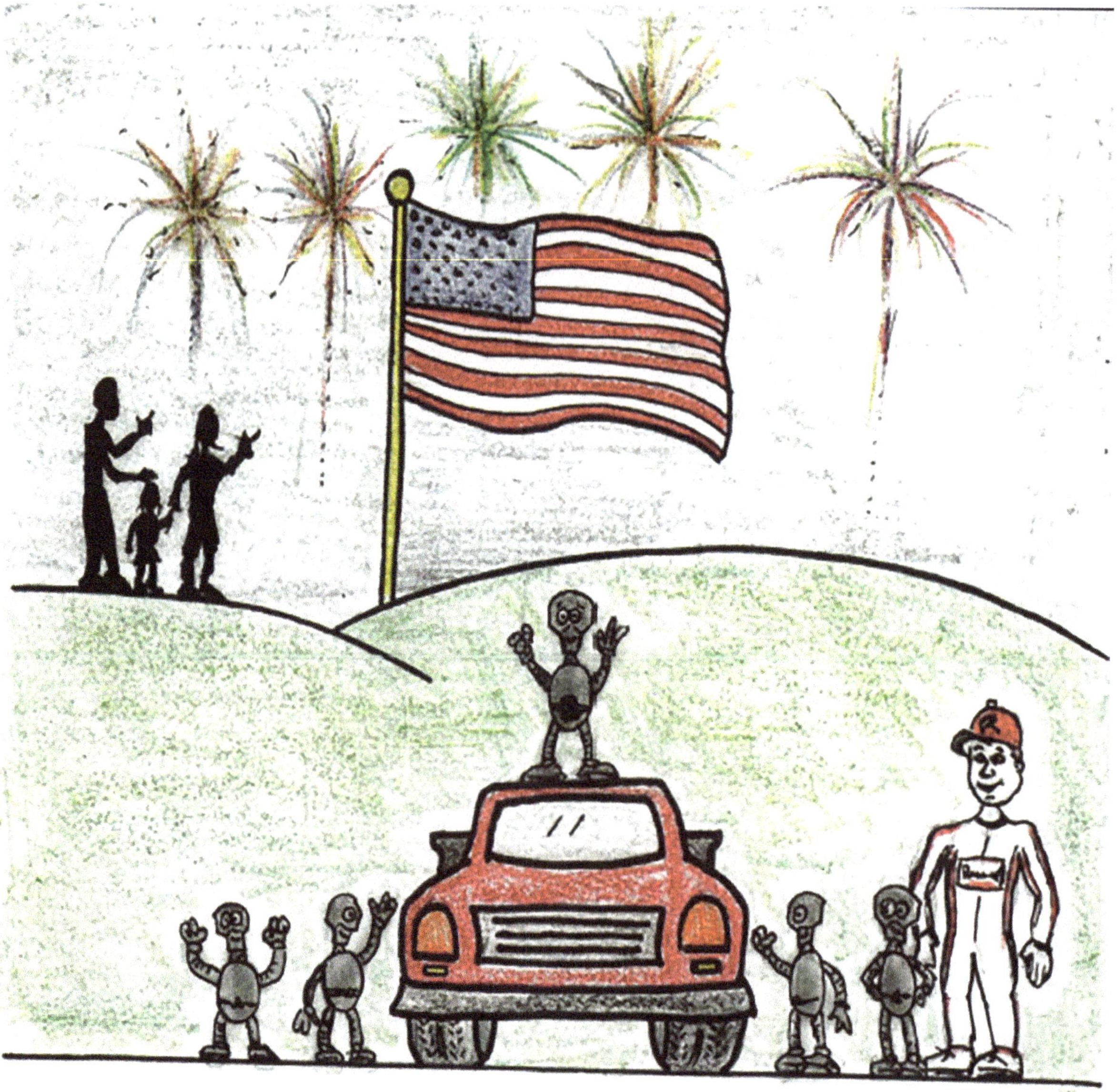

Ronnie Racecar was so happy that all the lug nuts were helping him. And guess what? This time Rusty was not just cheering for the other lug nuts. He was cheering for himself too, as part of the team.

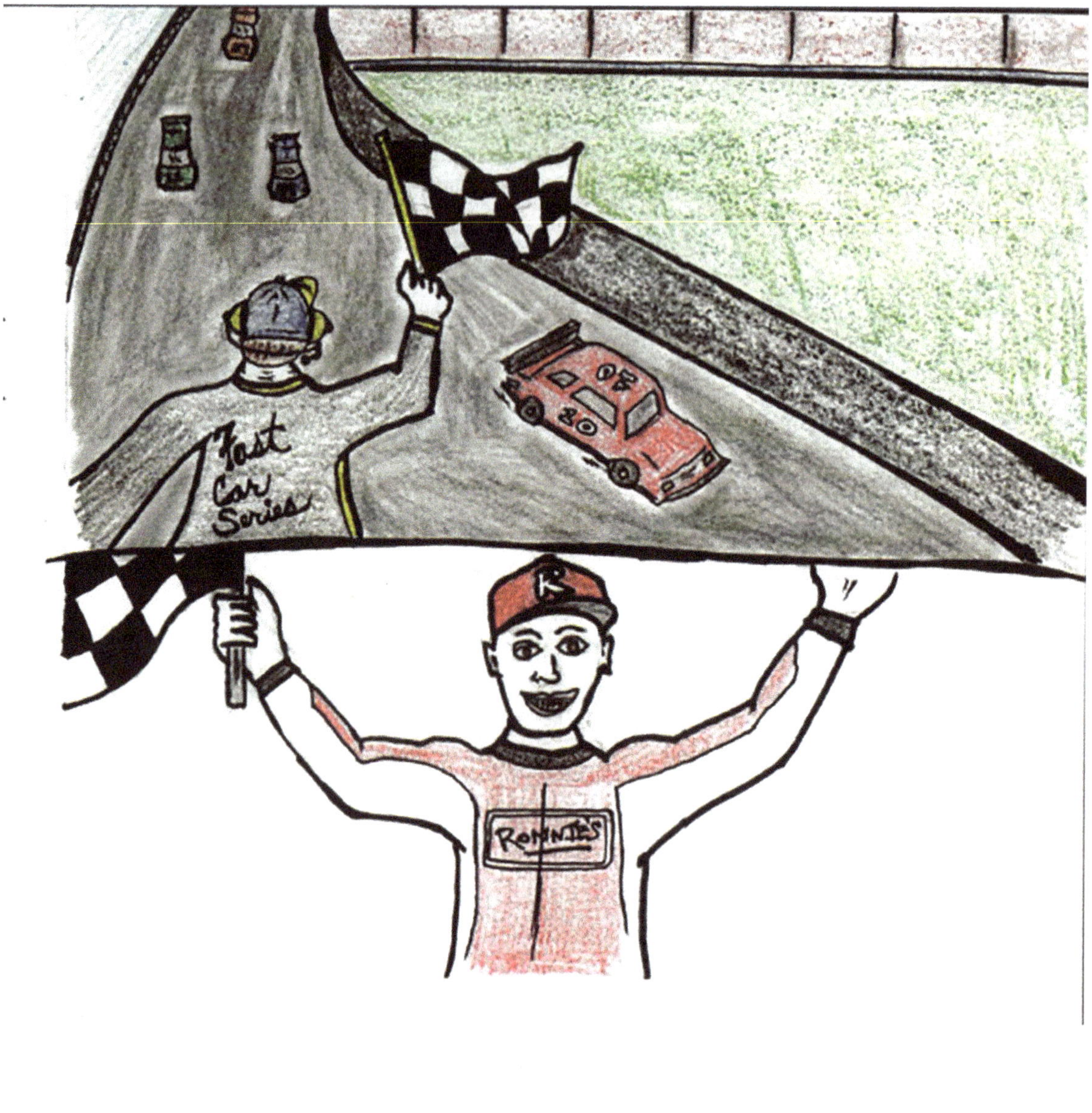
Fast Car Series
80

Ronnie's wheels went round and round and faster and faster, and when the checkered flag came out, Ronnie Race Car won the race that day. He was happy and proud.

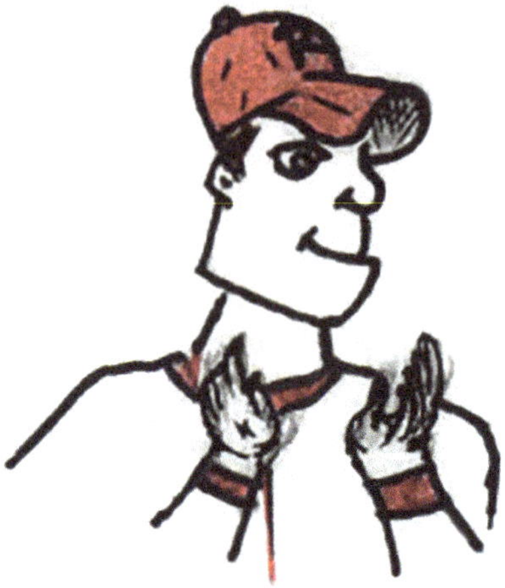

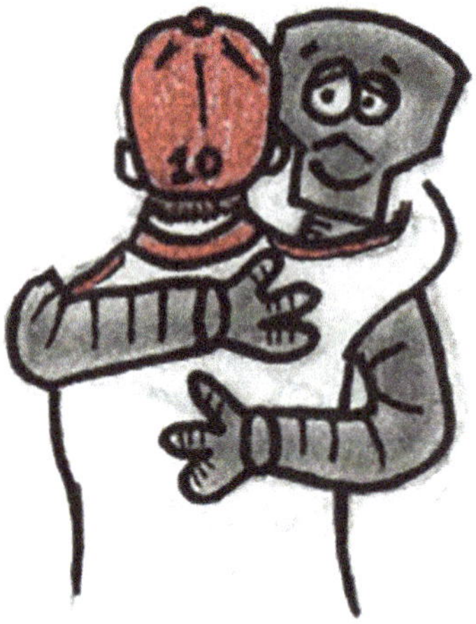
10

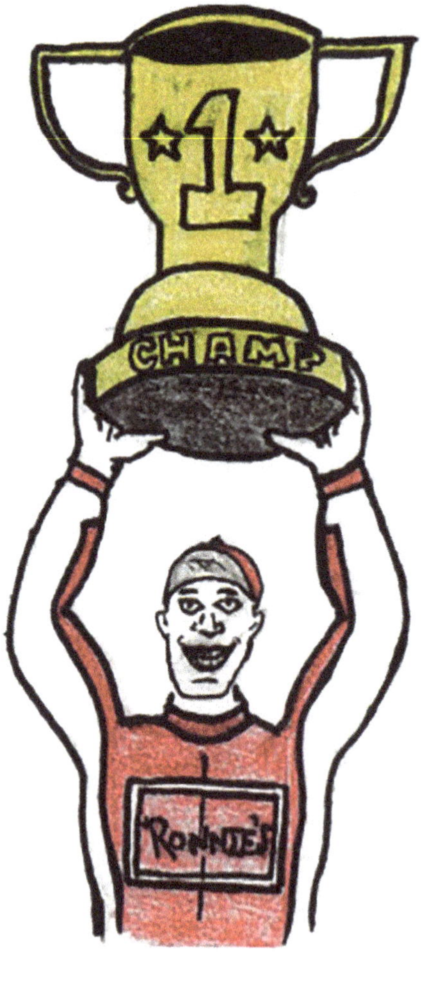
1
CHAMP
"RONNIE'S"

Ronnie Racecar and his pit crew learned a valuable lesson that day. Just because someone looks different than you, it does not mean they don't have something to offer to the team. Rusty wasn't brand-new or shiny, but he was patient and kind and liked being a part of the team, even if it meant just cheering for the others.

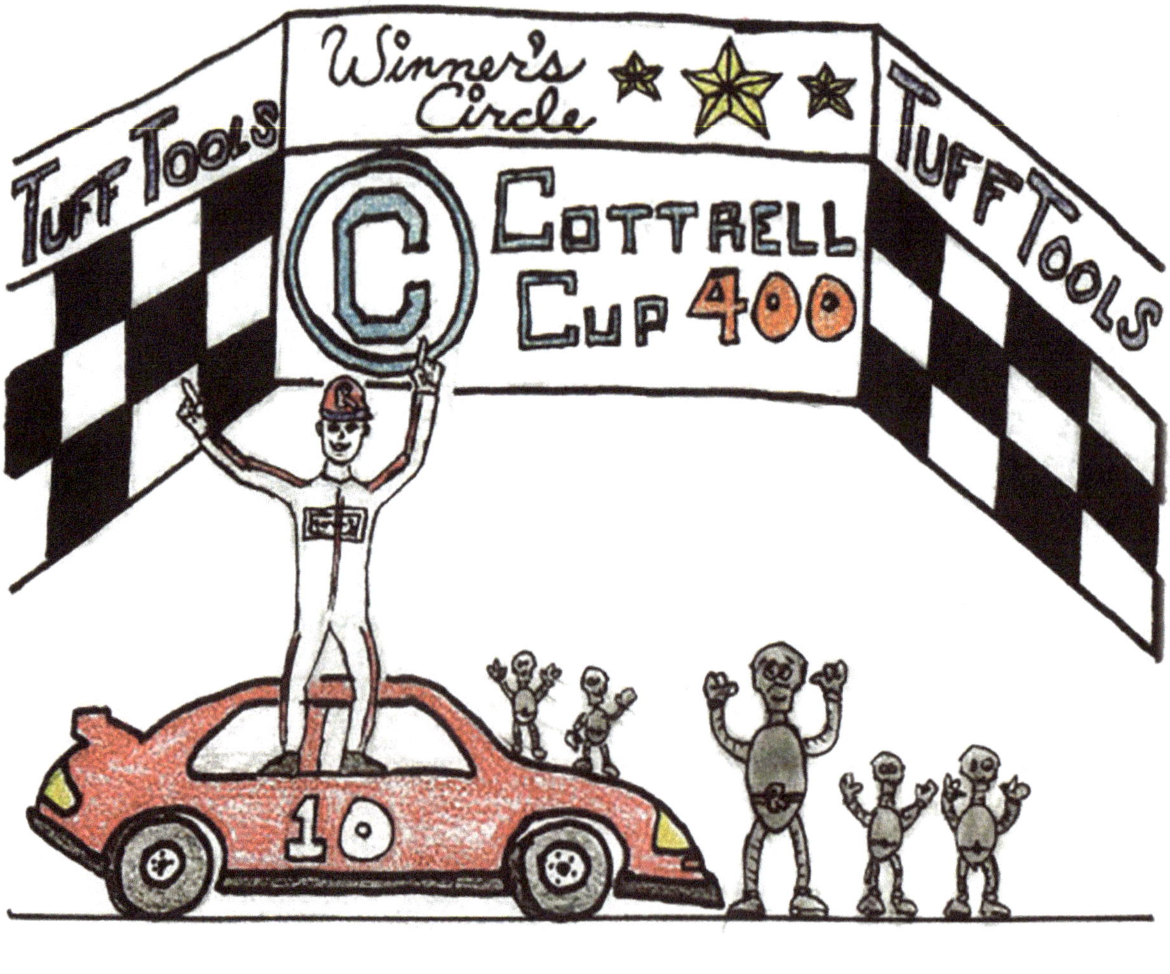
Winner's Circle
TUFF TOOLS
COTTRELL CUP 400
TUFF TOOLS
10

He was happy to help no matter what. Four shiny lug nuts would not be enough to make the wheel work right, but with five lug nuts, even though one was rusty, something great happened. Rusty was a part of a winning race team!

ABOUT THE AUTHOR

Ruth Blowers-Marquart has always had a passion for children and has spent time with kids in many capacities throughout her adult life. Ruth has a bachelor's degree in human development. She has worked in day care and preschool settings with typical children and children with special needs. She has also worked with teens with developmental disabilities and in human services where she worked with developmentally disabled adults and children, helping them reach their potential through services made available to them.

Ruth is from Geneva, New York, a small town in the Finger Lakes region. She lives with her husband Dana, as well as two dogs, Digger and Roscoe; one cat, Bailey, and a betta fish named Troy Aikman. She has two grown children, Adam (Amanda) and Kelsey (Jason), who also live in Geneva.

Ruth spends most of her days caring for her two grandchildren, Riley and Caiden. Ruth enjoys spending time with her family, baking endless amounts of cookies, reading, playing trivia, going to NASCAR races, and traveling to Florida when opportunity allows.

CPSIA information can be obtained
at www.ICGtesting.com
Printed in the USA
BVHW02s1115180818
524548BV00006B/22/P